Everybody Loves Leo

By Norris Bloom

ISBN (Print) 978-1-54390-315-7

Dedicated to **Smokin Joe**, **Bruno**, **Buster**, **Phoebe**, **Mojo**, **Zara**, **Snoop Dogg**, **Brutis**, **Remi**, **Leo**, and rescue dogs everywhere!

www.norrisbloom.com

Editor **Robert Norris**

http://www2.gol.com/users/norris/

Illustrator **Amruta Patil**

On Sunday, my mom came
into my bedroom and said,
"Wake up sleepyhead!
Rise and shine! You too, Leo.
It's time for vacation."

"Is Leo coming with us?" I asked.

"No," she said,"The hotel doesn't
allow pets, but don't worry.
Leo will be happy.
He is going to stay next
door with Miss Annie."

When our suitcases were packed, Dad said, "Let me take a picture of you and Leo." Then my mom's phone buzzed and she said, "Oh, no!"

"What's the matter?" I asked.

"Miss Annie has to go out of town for a few days during the week. Who will we get to watch Leo?"

"Leave it to me," Dad said and made some calls. "It's all settled. Leo is going to spend one day each with Walter, Aunt Michelle, Uncle Ronnie, and Grandma."

And I said, "Lucky for us, everybody loves Leo."

Mom said, "Look, Miss Annie took Leo
to the lake yesterday so he could have fun
in the water too. Miss Annie really loves Leo."
And I said, "Everybody loves Leo."

On Tuesday, we went on a long hike. When we reached the top of the steep hill, my dad's phone buzzed.

Dad said, "My friend Walter took his dog and Leo out for a walk today. Looks like Walter's dog Smokin Joe loves Leo."
And I said, "Everybody loves Leo."

Mom said, "Poor Leo. Aunt Michelle took him to be groomed, but the groomer said he was a very good dog and that she just loves Leo." And I said, "Everybody loves Leo."

Dad said, "Uncle Ronnie sent us a picture. It's raining at home too, so he and Leo are staying inside today. Uncle Ronnie sure loves Leo."
And I said, "Everybody loves Leo."

Mom laughed and said, "I hope Grandma doesn't give Leo too many treats. Grandma really loves Leo."
And I said, "Everybody loves Leo."

On Saturday, we packed up our suitcases and drove home. Miss Annie and Leo were waiting for us on the front porch, and Mom said, "Looks like Leo had a good vacation."

Draw or put a picture of your pet here.